Aunt Barbar
Tara Toodles
book!! Can yo
Thank you's
encouraging me
me!

Hello Morning

SATYA T. NELMS

Copyright © 2014 Satya Tara Nelms

Cover Design by Maggie Regan

All rights reserved.

ISBN-13: 978-1503049833

ISBN-10: 1503049833

For all those in search of themselves...

ACKNOWLEDGMENTS

The term "self-published" is somewhat misleading. It is true that I have had to do a lot on my own, but it is also true that I would be nowhere without the incredible support of friends and family who have doubled as beta readers, editors, web designers, photographers, artists, sounding boards and much more. First and foremost I would like to thank my wonderful husband, Isaiah, for his unwavering support. I'd also like to thank my children Isys, Naomi and Miles for providing me with the motivation to follow my dreams, so that I can lead by example and one day encourage them to follow theirs. I would also like to thank Patrice King, Errol King, Maggie Regan, Caryn McCarthy, Ryan McCarthy, Akasha Nelms, Dorie Taylor, Connie Cross, James McCarthy, Jeannine Osayande, Chenoa Osayande, Mandisa (Candace) Lee, Makeda Redmond, Ptah Osayande, Jevyn Nelms, Michelle Nicole, Olivia Lotz, Karlene Burrell-McRae and the most amazing grandmother a girl could ask for, Joan Robinson. I love you all so very much. Thank you for believing in me.

CHAPTER I

Aidan is home drunk again, and again I will have to pretend to be asleep. His keys jingle in the door, waking me. I silently curse myself for being a light sleeper and look over at the glowing red lights on the nightstand. 2:13am. I shut my eyes tight, but not too tight, slow my breathing, open my mouth ever so slightly, and let my muscles go limp. I lay there willing my body not to betray me. I hear a slight thud against the floor, just before he slides into bed behind me. I can tell from the way my nightgown lifts off my skin ever so´ slightly and adheres to him that

1

every stitch of his clothing is lying in a pile next to the bed.

I keep my breath even, but I can do nothing about my racing heart. When he begins to hike up my nightgown, I garble some unintelligible sound, and roll a little closer to the edge of the bed, hoping signs of my nocturnal habits will turn him off, but he doesn't stop. His hand slips down the back of my underwear.

"Babe?" I whisper

"Hmm." He groans.

"What time is it?" I croak, attempting to distract him.

His only response is to slide my underwear further down my thighs.

Before I feel the soft cotton hit the back of my kneecaps, I begin to squirm.

"I'm tired." I make every effort to keep my voice strong and assertive.

"Shhh," he says as he clenches my shoulder to brace himself and slams into me.

"Please. No." I beg him, my confidence shattered.

My pleas fall on deaf ears and he continues.

I lay there silent and stiff with the sheets balled up in my fists. Tears run down my cheeks, and over his fingers like mini waterfalls, as I wait for it to be over.

He gives one last low grunt, and with an over exuberant thrust of his hips, it's done. He throws his thigh over my body and falls asleep still inside of me.

I wait until his body grows heavy and I slip off of the bed down to the floor, releasing myself. I look over my shoulder at him, sleeping like the dead, and I crawl out of our bedroom door, still ajar from when he entered. Once I'm in the hallway I stand up and slide along the wall to the bathroom.

I push the door shut trying not to make a sound, and lock the door with equal care. I wrap my arms tight around my body, and begin to sob.

Water from the shower pours down onto my bare shoulders. I sit over the drain and watch the pool forming around my toes. I tuck my chin to my chest and press my knees to the top of my head. My belly rises and my back arches and falls with each breath. The rhythm is deceiving. So calm and steady.

How did I get here? I remember the first time it happened. I remember not even realizing what had happened until it was already over. I remember the way I scooted as close to the edge of my side of the bed as I could; I curled so tightly in on myself that my joints ached. I stared at the same corner of the room for hours. I watched the way it changed as the light shifted and night begrudgingly gave way to day. I remember squeezing my eyes shut when I heard him stirring beside me. I remember the feeling of his eyes on me, as he checked to see if I was awake. I remember the way I froze when he touched me on the forehead, gently whispering, telling me I was going to be late for work. I remember being confused by him acting so normal; had I imagined the night before? I remember releasing my extremities when he left, and rolling onto my back. I stared at the stark canvas of the ceiling, and began to weave the tale that would allow me to stay. *He doesn't know what he did. He must have been really drunk. He's never done that before. Maybe he didn't hear me say stop. Maybe I didn't say it loud enough. That must be it. It was just a misunderstanding. It's not like he ra--. It's not like he meant to hurt me.* And just like that I'd convinced myself of a lie in face of stark reality.

I raise my head, close my eyes and let the water tap a beat on my lids. After a breath to steady myself, I grope the tiled walls, turn off the water and step out into a cloud of steam.

I drag my palm across the foggy mirror and stare back at my reflection. She looks like me. But is she me? As the water begins to dry, my tear stains become more pronounced. I pull the black elastic hair tie from my wrist and gather up my curls on the crown of my head. I splash my face with cool water hoping to stir some life, but I am numb. And somehow, I am here.

I look at my underwear and nightgown lying in a heap next to the toilet like they have betrayed me. I pick them up and toss them in the garbage. I open the linen closet and pull out a pair of sweatpants and a t-shirt from my secret stash I started compiling when it became apparent that Aidan was going to make a habit of these late night rendezvous.

I tiptoe down the hall and peek into our bedroom. He's got one leg dangling off the edge of my side of the bed, and he's started to snore. I pull the door shut until it's only open a crack.

The water pitcher is practically empty. I scowl at the empty air. I look up at the clock on the wall 4:00am, too late to go back to sleep now. So, I fill the kettle up from the tap, and take down a fresh pouch of chamomile tea from the cupboard, hoping it will do something for my nerves.

I pace back and forth in front of the stove, not wanting to be far when the whistle blows. When steam begins to rush out of the spout, I remove it from the flame before it can sound its alarm, and pour the hot water into my cup.

I curl up in my favorite chair and stare out of the window. The Hudson River is calm and serene. Lights twinkle on the Jersey shoreline as I sip my tea. When I get to the bottom of the cup, I place it on the coffee table beside me, and lean my head against the back of the chair. I close my eyes and send silent prayers to every known God and a few I have created, begging them for clarity, for hope, and for deliverance from this familiar pain. Before I have time to stop myself, I fall asleep.

"Shae? Shae baby it's 8 o'clock. You're gonna be late for work."

I wake up to Aidan's big brown eyes and pearly white teeth smiling down at me. I uncurl my legs and plant my feet on the floor. I roll my shoulders back, and stretch my arms above my head.

Aidan plants a kiss on my forehead, turns and heads for the kitchen.

"Why'd you go to sleep out here?"

"You were drunk when you came home."

"Sorry babe, I went out with some colleagues after work and got a little carried away."

"That's the seventh time in the last 3 months that you've gotten 'a little carried away.'"

"Aw, come on Shae, it's not like I'm an alcoholic or something. I know you're grumpy from sleeping out in the chair but gimme a break. Was I snorin' or somethin'? Is that why you came out here?"

My voice drops to barely above a whisper.

"You did it again."

He freezes.

"Did what again?"

I turn to look at him, but I can barely make eye contact. He hangs his head.

I turn and look back out of the window.

"I'm sorry baby, I know that must be really uncomfortable for you..."

I whip my head around.

"Uncomfortable?" I scowl at him. "Uncomfortable!"

"Take it easy."

"Take it easy? I said no Aidan. I said no! And you didn't stop."

"Hold up now, what are you tryna say?"

"I'm saying you came into our bed drunk off your ass, and..."

Aidan comes around the kitchen island. He clenches his fists, and his lips turn up into a cold sneer.

"And what Shae? And what?"

"I..."

He's so close to me now I can feel the anger rolling off of him in waves.

"I can't believe this shit."

He backs away from me and storms down the hallway.

"Ain't this a way to start the day." His voice echoes off the walls.

I hear a door slam, and then the sound of breaking glass. I'm frozen in my spot for what feels like entirely too long. Then I make a run for it. I dash around the corner into my bedroom, snatch my wallet off the dresser, slip on the flip flops at the end of my bed, and make a beeline for the door. I snatch my keys from the hook and I'm gone.

Rush hour pedestrian traffic fills the streets, and I slip easily into the throng on Broadway. Despite my state of dress, no one looks at me, no one attempts to make eye contact, and I let the crowd take me. My body moves on auto-pilot and my mind goes blank. I don't want to think. Don't want to feel. I just want to walk until my legs give out.

The crowd starts to thin around Lincoln Center, and I reach instinctively for my pocket to look at my phone and check the time. I dig down deep into the crevices coming up with nothing more than lint balls. I frantically check my other pocket, but I already know where it is. Sitting on the nightstand, nestled in its charger. Damn!

I spot a pay phone near the subway station and deposit some change from the pouch in my wallet.

I punch in a few numbers, and wait.

"Good morning! Idlewild Talent and Literary Agency, how may I help you?" Mina's sweet, melodic voice greets me.

"Good morning Mina." I throw every ounce of energy I have into sounding bright and cheery.

"Oh, hi Shae! Good morning."

"I'm having a bit of a family emergency and I'm not going to be able to come in today."

"Oh, I'm so sorry to hear that."

"Thanks Mina."

"Hold on, a sec."

"Ok."

"Lily's stepped away from her desk for a second, so let me bring up your schedule."

"Great."

"Alright. Looks like you've got a staff meeting, and a couple of phone conferences... of course I can have Lily reschedule those, but, nothing too serious. So, I'll have Lily postpone those meetings, and you should be all set."

"Sounds good. I'll see you tomorrow Mina."

"See you tomorrow Shae!"

I hang up the phone and my hand lingers on the receiver. My hand tightens around it, and I hang my head. *You will not call him Shae. Back away from the phone.* I turn on my heel, and let my feet do the thinking.

Central Park in the summer time. The grass is green, the trees have fully blossomed, and the air smells almost fresh. If you go deep enough into its winding paths, you could almost forget you're in the city. Almost. Rest assured a crazy taxi driver looking for a short cut to midtown will race by when you least expect it, taking years off of your life, just to remind you of where you are. Until then, feel free to get lost in the magic of it all.

I sit in the shade of an unclaimed tree and roll my sweatpants up to my knees. I tilt my head back and watch as the birds flutter back and forth between the branches. I let myself live in this moment just for a second, because I know the questions are coming. I briefly indulge fantasies of an urban Swiss Family Robinson, nestled in the heart of the city.

A brown mare trots along a path in the distance. I can just make out the couple in the carriage it pulls. Their faces are close together but they aren't kissing. They look so... intimate. Their moment interrupts mine, and I feel my body closing in on itself. It starts in my chest, and rises up to my throat, until it stunts my breath. I feel dizzy. What am I going to do?

My palms grow clammy, and I feel sweat beads accumulating at my temples. The more my breath quickens, the more anxious I become, but the more anxious I am the more difficult it is to slow my breathing. It's a vicious cycle. My nostrils feel constricted, no matter how much air I try to bring in it's still not enough. I look around me. Is anyone seeing this? Can anyone feel my panic? Am I causing a scene? If I pass out right now will anyone even notice? I concentrate on each person that passes me from the path that crosses my tree. I stare at them, hoping they will feel my eyes and acknowledge that I am here.

An older gentleman glances in my direction. It worked! The sides of his lips curl up into a smile, his eyes warm, and he inclines his head in a silent gesture of greeting. I return his smile with what probably comes off as more of an awkward grimace. He returns to his own thoughts, and continues down the path.

He couldn't tell! The concentration it took to make him look and my successful deception seem to quiet my pulse, but the aftershocks ripple through my body. My heart beat still bounces off the walls inside my head, and I can feel a headache creeping up behind my eyes.

I inch closer to the tree, and lean my head back until it kisses the bark. I cross my legs and place my hands, palm side down, on my knees. The proud city girl inside of me shakes her head at me in indignation, but I shut her out and close my eyes. I bring two fingers to my wrist to remind myself that my heart is not beating nearly as fast as I think it is, and then focus on my breath.

I first started having anxiety attacks when I was a child. The first one was just after my first choir solo in middle school. I'd sung in front of my church before, but this felt different. I got up in front of my whole school, closed my eyes, waited for the piano cue, opened my mouth and sang. I didn't open my eyes again until I'd let the last note go. I listened to the piano trail off and close the ballad, and then there was silence.

Maybe it was the boy in the seventh row back, first seat on the right that I had a crush on, watching me intently. Maybe it was Sherri Johnson sitting front and center who loved telling me, "You think you're better than somebody cuz you're light skinned and got good hair, well you ain't." Or maybe it was my mama with her jaw set, passing judgment on every note that stepped a toe off-key, 'cause she wasn't gonna have me up there embarrassin' her. Whatever it was, the quiet went on a moment too long for me, and I ran off the stage.

When a teacher found me a few hours later, I was huddled in the third floor bathroom stall, the front of my white blouse transparent from being drenched in sweat, and my black pants stuck to me like they were lined with adhesive. I had one hand on my head and the other gripping my chest as I looked up into her eyes and said, "I'm having a heart attack." She scooped me up in her arms, and rushed me down the hall to the school nurse.

Nurse Liles was a pretty woman. She was a beautiful deep brown color and wore her hair in a short pixie cut. Her breasts were small but perky, and her hips, backside and thighs seemed to explode out from her itty-bitty waist. Boys 6th grade through 8th and even some teachers feigned illness just to spend a few quiet moments alone with her, but she paid them no mind at all.

As I lay there on the table looking up at her I swore she radiated sunshine. She was my angel, come to save me. My eyes fixed on her full pouty lips doused in red lipstick as she spoke to me. Even her breath was sweet.

"Shae. I'm Nurse Liles."

I smiled shyly like I didn't know who she was.

"How are you feelin' sweetie?"

"My heart is beating too fast, and I feel kinda dizzy."

She placed a stethoscope on my chest and listened. Then she took it out of her ears, and wrapped it around her neck. She held one end of it in each of her hands.

"I hear you had a big solo in the school concert today."

"Yeah."

"I hear you were amazing, the audience was clappin' and cheerin'."

"No they weren't. You're just trying to make me feel better."

"No ma'am. I'm telling the truth. You were a hit!"

I drop my eyes away from hers.

"I guess I didn't stay long enough to see that."

"Yeah, I heard about that too. What happened?"

"I don't really know. I just looked out into the crowd and all these faces were staring back at me, and I just couldn't be there anymore."

While I'm talking Nurse Liles has taken one of my hands in hers and has two fingers pressed against my pulse.

"How you feeling now, Shae?"

I stop and assess the situation. The sweat on my body has gone cold.

"I'm still a little dizzy, but I think my heart has gone back to normal. How'd you do that?"

"Have you ever felt like this before?"

"No, nothing like this has ever happened to me before. Was it a heart attack?"

Nurse Liles chuckled.

"Shae, what you just experienced is called an anxiety attack."

"What's that?"

"Sometimes under extremely stressful situations, people's nervous systems go into overdrive. The result can lead to chest palpitations, hot and cold flashes and disorientation. I'm guessing seeing all of those people staring at you sent your body into a panic."

I sat up on the Nurse's table.

"How do I keep it from happening again?"

"You can do your best to stay calm, and take slow, deep breaths if you find yourself feeling anxious."

"Anything else?"

"If you start having frequent anxiety attacks you could meet with a therapist to discuss other options, but that's something you'd have to discuss with your parents."

Horrifying visions of telling my mother I need to see a therapist flashed through my mind. I saw her standing there, one hand on her hip, eyes narrowed, "Therapy? What do you need therapy for? You can't be goin' out into the street tellin' all this family's business." I shook my head. "Stay calm. Slow deep breaths. Got it."

I slid my legs around until they were dangling over the side of the table.

"You sure you're ready to go back to class."

"Yup."

Nurse Liles bit the corner of her bottom lip and looked at me hard. "Promise me you'll come back and see me if this happens again."

"Sure." I said a little too quickly and hopped off the table.

"I mean it Shae."

I turned and looked Nurse Liles in the eye. "I promise I'll come back if this happens again."

And with that I made my way to 5th Period English.

The ground beneath my butt suddenly feels a lot harder than when I first sat down. I open my eyes and shift from one cheek to the other. The attack has passed, but I can tell it's been there from the dull ache in my muscles. I stretch my arms up over my head, and press my shoulder blades together until I hear a small crack. My eyes take a moment to adjust to the bright mid-morning sun.

No one new crosses my path and I decide it's time to move on. The blood rushes to my head as I jump up to standing. I steady myself with a hand on the tree. When I look down the path in either direction, neither looks particularly promising. I check to make sure no one is looking and indulge myself in a good old fashioned game of eeny-meeny-miney-mo, a tried and true means of decision making going back no doubt to the dawn of time. Right it is.

SATYA NELMS

CHAPTER II

My feet fall into a rhythm, and soon I am on auto-pilot. The thoughts in my head are the usual white noise clutter you hear when you're trying to still your mind. *What meetings did I miss today. What do I have on my agenda for the rest of the week? Oo! Those flowers are pretty. I wonder if I could grow those at home. Maybe I should take that gardening workshop in the park next weekend.* And on, and on. Then the heavy hitters start to drift in. *When am I going to go home? I can't wander around the park forever. Will Aidan be home when I get there? What will he say? What will I say? How will the two of us be able to go on after this morning?*

I try to do like they tell me in meditation class and let the thoughts pass like clouds in the sky. I try my hardest to disappear in the space between the thoughts, but peace and tranquility will not come easy today. The weight of my musings makes me feel weary, and I look for a place to sit. I stagger over to the nearest bench, and collapse rather than sit down.

My breath begins to pick up the pace and I scold myself. No! Not again. *Breathing in, I'm breathing in. Breathing out, I'm breathing out.* I fill my belly with air on my inhale, and try to release my pain on my exhale.

My eyes dart first one-way and then another, willing a sign to appear and offer me some direction. I heard somewhere that when we look for signs, we really already know the way we ought to go, or at least the way we want to go. We're just looking for some external validation. I have no such inclinations in this moment.

So I look out in front of me. I allow the full weight of my situation to descend upon me. I let it consume me, because I have no other viable alternatives right now, nothing to distract me. I give myself over to the pain for lack of better options.

Tears form a film over my eyes and blur my vision. The park becomes a stained glass window of fuzzy shapes and colors. I listen to my heartbeat thump. I feel it pound at my temples. My tears and I come to an impasse. I will not let them fall and they cannot retreat.

"Miss?" A voice breaks my concentration. My eyes take advantage of the weakness and a tear falls from each of my eyes. The world comes back into focus.

A woman stands before me slightly crouched over with her eyes narrowed. She's a young woman around my age, average height, with deep brown skin and corkscrew curls springing from her head every which way. She moves them out of her eyes when she leans in to speak to me.

"Miss, are you all right?"

I part my lips as though to respond but no sound comes out. She chews at the corner of her lip and looks off down the path. She glances down at the watch on her wrist.

She straightens up, and starts to back away from me. Something inside of me panics. For some reason unbeknownst to me, I don't want her to leave.

"I'm not alright." I whisper.

She stops. Did she hear me?

"I'm not alright." I say again. I shake my head back and forth and repeat it once again, more to myself than to this woman. "I'm not alright."

She takes tentative steps, approaching me like a wild animal she's afraid of spooking. She places a hand, palm side down on the bench next to me.

"Is it alright if I sit here?"

I nod. My voice seems to have gone back into hiding. My tears on the other hand, have taken complete advantage of my preoccupation with this woman, and are flowing freely. She sits next to me in silence for a few moments. She is looking straight ahead, just like me.

"My name is Kiera."

"My name is Shae."

"That's such a cool name."

"Thank you." I feign a smile through my tears.

Kiera lifts her hand up from her lap, and then puts it back down. She turns her head and looks at me. I see her out of the corner of my eye, but I don't move. She lifts her hand back up, and takes one of my hands in hers. She looks forward again. I squeeze her hand. My head drops and my shoulders shake with the heave of my sobs.

My words tumble out in fits and starts. Keira turns to look at me, but she does not interrupt.

"I don't know how I got here. I'm sitting on a park bench next to a stranger, balling my eyes out."

I turn to look at Keira. "This isn't me... I mean I am not this person."

She cocks her head to the side and looks at me quizzically. "What person might that be?"

"A person without a plan. A person who has nowhere to turn. A person who lets her boyfriend..."

"A person who lets her boyfriend what?"

I take a deep sigh. I bite my lower lip so hard I nearly draw blood.

"Have you ever had something you know... and you know you know it, but you still can't say it out loud, cause that would make it real, and you just can't stand to bring it into the world... to make it real?"

A look of understanding flits across her eyes and her brow furrows. "I've had something like that before, yeah... but sometimes bringing it into the real world is the only way you can begin to deal with it."

"I think some part of me knows that, but fixing my mouth to say the words is something else entirely."

"Maybe I can help?"

I look back down at my lap. "How?"

"Why don't you tell me how you and your boyfriend met... start from the beginning, and then we can make our way to how you got here... that sound ok?"

"Yeah, but if you don't mind me asking... why are you doing this? You don't even know me."

Kiera leans back against the park bench and looks up at the sky. Her curls bounce with each movement. She rakes her fingers through her scalp and gathers her hair in a fist at the crown of her head. She purses her lips and turns back to me.

"To be honest, I don't really know. When you live in the city, you're trained not to notice people. You learn not to see the homeless people lining the streets, or the panhandlers on the subway platform. You learn to mind your business, and treat things outside your bubble with concentrated indifference, but, for whatever reason, that has always been hard for me."

She squeezes my hand.

"I stopped because I noticed you. I stopped because something about your pain felt raw and familiar, and I couldn't imagine continuing on like I hadn't seen you."

"Oh."

Kiera smiles. "Is that a good enough reason?"

I return her smile. "Sounds like a good reason to me."

"All righty then... so about this boyfriend..."

"You sure you have time for this?"

She winks at me.

"One of the perks of being your own boss."

I laugh, and am surprised by the sound.

"Must be nice."

"It has its advantages."

She shoves my shoulder lightly. In a matter of minutes we have assumed the intimacy of old friends.

"Stop stallin' and get to it," Kiera tells me.

"You caught that huh?"

"Yeah I did."

"Alright, alright... How did I meet Aidan?"

"The boyfriend's name is Aidan?"

"Yup."

"Cool. Yes, how did you meet Aidan?"

"We met in Sociology my freshmen year. He was a nice guy. He was one of those guys that looks good on paper, ya know? At the time, I actually had a boyfriend, another jerk... I confided in Aidan. Not just about the boyfriend, but about everything. About my life growing up with my mom... stuff I'd never told anybody, and he would say the sweetest things..."

I bite my lip to stifle a surge of emotion.

"He'd tell me how I deserved to be treated better, and he told me I was beautiful and amazing, and I needed to hear those things. Looking back on it now, I think he knew I needed to hear those things. I don't know that he ever meant a single word."

A curious look passes over Kiera's face. "Why do you say that?" she asks.

"Once things with my boyfriend ended, Aidan was there waiting in the wings, and falling out of one relationship and into another, didn't feel too fast, it felt natural. But once we got together, everything changed."

I chew on the corner of my mouth. "You know, when Aidan and me were friends, when I was with him, talking to him, that was the first time I felt safe, so when things started to fall apart with him, I just kinda resigned myself to this hopelessness. I figured if a guy like Aidan..."

"What do you mean a guy like Aidan?"

"I mean a guy everybody likes. I mean the guy that professors loved, had tons of friends, half the campus wanted to be with him. He's smart, and beautiful... If someone like that could do the things... I just don't see how or why I should think there's someone better. So, I guess I stay because I figure it could be worse, and I don't really have faith that it could be better."

I pause a moment. "We weren't always like this. *He* wasn't always like this."

"Like what Shae?" Kiera nudges gently.

I continue as though I haven't even heard Kiera. It's almost like I'm talking to myself. "When we finally decided to start dating, it was so easy... like slipping into sweatpants after a long day in a business suit, but then..." I stop and purse my lips.

"But then what?"

"But then he stopped being my friend. It's like my friend Aidan and my boyfriend Aidan were two different people."

"How so?"

"After we'd been dating a little while he started having all these ideas about what a girlfriend should be...what I should be. So many of his sentences started with, "No girlfriend of mine would ever...""

"Would ever what?"

"Dress like that, talk like that, stay out that late, dance like that at a party. The list could go on forever. It got to feel like nothing I did, nothing I was, was good enough, and I ended up in this place where I feel..."

"Empty."

"No. No, I feel lucky." My chest heaves as all the pain of the last few hours pours into my words. "I feel lucky that he still wants to be with me. That with all my flaws he still wants me. That he puts up with my many shortcomings, except I didn't know they were shortcomings until he told me they were. I feel. Lucky."

I turn to Kiera. "When I was growing up, it was always just me and my mom. Nobody else." I shift on the bench away from Kiera and stare out ahead of me. "I'd ask my mother where my father was, and she'd tell me, 'he left us.' That was it, no other details except for the colorful names she liked to call him. I'd ask about grandparents, aunts, uncles, cousins, and she gave me all these stories about how this person was untrustworthy, and that person had betrayed her, and the other one was chronically unreliable. One by one, she gave me an excuse for why these people weren't in her life... weren't in my life. You would think that would have hardened me... would have made me really suspicious of everyone in my life, but it didn't."

My words get caught in my throat, then trickle out in fits and starts. "I always wanted people to like me. I'd meet a person and the next day, I'd be calling them my best friend. And if they weren't the nicest people, or if they did something to hurt me, I just accepted it. I grew up believing that that's what people do. I mean that's what everyone had done to my mother, and she made sure I knew I wasn't special. I expect people to hurt me. I expect love to hurt."

I stop a moment to process these words, these words that were nothing but half formed feelings up until a moment ago. Then, I continue in barely more than a whisper and Kiera must strain to hear me.

"So, I feel lucky. I feel lucky to be with someone who criticizes me more than he compliments me. I feel lucky to be with someone who berates me like a child. I feel lucky to be with someone who comes home drunk and rapes me twice a month, because at least he's still here... at least he hasn't left me."

"Shae, what did you just say?"

"He rapes me. I said he rapes me." And just like that my words make it real. "I hear him stumble into the house and I know it's coming. So, I lay there and squeeze my eyes shut and pretend to be asleep. And when that doesn't work, I ask him, I beg him not to. And when that doesn't work I press my thighs together, sure that nothing but the jaws of life will pry them apart. And when that doesn't work, because none of it ever does, I lay there frozen, clutching the sheets to brace myself and wait for it to be over."

I look over at Kiera and her face is covered in tears I never heard fall. *When did she shed the first*, I wonder absently. *What pushed her over the edge?*

I become aware of the energy this exposition has cost me and I am all at once exhausted. My shoulders drop and my chin dips forward, "I have to go home." My words are laced with a heady combination of fatigue and defeat.

"You can't go back there." Kiera barely keeps the horror in her voice in check.

"I have nowhere else to go."

"You can come home with me."

"Really? You would let a perfect stranger come home with you?"

"Perfect stranger?" Kiera wipes her tears with the back of her hand. "Girl, we're practically family now." She chuckles.

I smile. "That's sweet of you, but say I do come home with you... then what? I can't stay forever, and my whole life is in that house. Childhood pictures, work files, high school yearbook, my cell phone... I've gotta go back sometime."

"None of that stuff matters, Shae."

"That stuff is my life..." I hang my head and grab handfuls of my hair. "We never stayed anywhere for very long when I was growing up. I got really good at packing, and even better at packing light. I don't hold on to much, so the things I hold onto count...They matter. You can't ask me to give those up too... I've given up so much already."

"Ok, ok, I get that. You've gotta go back at some point, but some point, doesn't need to be today. You don't even have a plan! What if he's there when you go back? How is that gonna work out?"

Keira looks at me and sees all of her unanswered questions reflected in my eyes. I stare at her blankly. She starts up again.

"You're right, we are strangers, but if you're not gonna come home with me, there's gotta be somewhere else you can go."

There is a long pause. Kiera hopes I am running through my mental address book, but something in my eyes indicates otherwise.

"Do you have people in your life who would have your back no matter what? People who you wouldn't give a second thought to telling pretty much anything?" I surprise her with my question.

"Uh, yeah. I mean not a ton of people, but yeah, I have a few people like that."

"And would you say those people know you pretty well?"

Kiera lets a nervous laugh trill through the air, uncertain where my line of questioning is going. "Probably better than I know myself."

"I have no one like that."

"Oh, come on, you've gotta have at least one person, there can't be…"

"I grew up with a lot of rules, but there was one in particular that my mother made sure I never forgot."

"What was that?"

"Never let anyone know what goes on inside this house. She made it very clear that I was not to run the streets telling people our 'family business.' And the few times I slipped, she made sure I regretted it"

I chew on my lip and take a breath before continuing. "Those few people you say you have, not a ton, but a few... I have no one like that. No one knows me well enough. I don't know that I know me well enough."

I have stunned Kiera speechless "No one knows about Aidan. If I'm being honest, I think the only reason I told you is precisely because I don't know you. You don't know me, you don't know Aidan... What's the likelihood that I'll ever see you again after today unless it's on purpose? Telling you feels safe."

"Telling me means nothing has to change."

"Unless I want it to."

Do I want this to change anything? Would it honestly be easier at this point to go back home, and pretend this never happened? Pretend I didn't say the things I said. Pretend I didn't just admit the things I've admitted to, to someone I've never met. Pretend I never ran away.

Doing that would mean more nights spent sitting on the shower floor watching the water pool around the drain, wondering if my life is headed in the same direction. I think about the way I feel after that brief moment when I wake up and forget for a split second what has happened. My throat closes in on itself, and I'm never sure if I'm going to suffocate or vomit. No, nothing about staying would be easy, but at least it is a familiar pain.

"Shae, you still with me."

I don't know how long I have been sitting here weighing bits of my life on some arbitrary scale. I look into Keira's eyes, long enough for her to worry I suppose.

"I'm still here. I do want things to change. But, I have to go back. I can't run from this. "

"There is a difference between running away and walking away."

"I would be running. I at least know myself well enough to know that."

"Why is that a bad thing?"

"Because when I run away, I don't even bother to look back over my shoulder. I leave it all in my rear view mirror. I don't think about where I'm going or how I'll get there, I just start running, and before I know it, I'm back where I started because I was so busy running away, I didn't notice I was running in a circle, and I can't end up back here again."

"So then walk away Shae! Walk away with both eyes open!"

"I can't do that until I say the words to him."

"Say what words to who?"

"To Aidan. I need to say them... say what I said to you, to him. I need to make it so we can't go back to what we were. Without those words he'll apologize, and I'll paint this picture for myself about how he's not really a bad guy, I mean everybody's got their flaws right, and I'll say okay. But he'll do it again, just like he has before, and nothing will change. I have to say the words."

Kiera just stares at me. "You said you left your phone, right?"

"Yeah"

She rummages through her purse, and starts emptying its contents on the bench between us. Lotion, cell phone, sunglasses, tissues, lip balm. Finally she produces a piece of paper and a pen. She tears the paper in half, and scrawls something on it. She hands me the blank half.

"Address and phone number."

I blink and tilt my head to the side. She offers an explanation.

"I want you to call me tomorrow. If you don't call me, I will call you. If you don't answer, I'm gonna pop by and make sure you're ok."

"You don't have to do that."

"Yes I do, Shae. Address and phone number."

I sigh and take the blank piece of paper and pen from her. I hand it over. She takes her half of the paper, gives it to me, and then encircles my closed fist between her hands.

"This happened, Shae, do you hear me? This conversation, this happened."

My breath gets caught in my chest and I nod.

CHAPTER III

I stand outside my apartment with the key in the door, but I don't turn it. I stand eerily still, listening for signs of life inside. When I left Kiera at the park it was 2:30pm, it should only be 3:00pm at the latest now. He shouldn't be home, but I don't want any surprises. So, I wait. When I am greeted with not so much as the creak of a floorboard I enter.

The mug from my tea this morning still sits on the coffee table. An open box of cereal sits on the kitchen counter next to a carton of milk. I give the box a shake. Empty. The cabinet the cereal was retrieved from is half open. I close it. I think about putting everything away, but I can't. Somehow the mundane remains of our broken morning routine serve as a reminder of what happened here.

My flip-flops slap against the hardwood floor and I walk into my bedroom. The covers lay bunched at the foot of the bed, and our bedroom mirror is in shards at the base of our dresser. So that's what broke. I move to take my cell phone from the charger, and it's no longer there. Upon further inspection I find it, screen cracked, strewn amidst a kaleidoscope of glass in various shapes and sizes.

I drop to my knees and attempt to pick up the pieces. I start with my phone. I tap the power button, trying to will the screen to light. Nothing. I hold down the button. Nothing. Take the battery out; put it back in. Nothing. I feel a lump form in my throat. My hands shake. I place the phone back in the charger, telling myself it just needs to charge again. Funny how my sanity hinges on something as simple as a phone.

I drop back to my knees and begin again. I make a basket out of the billowy fabric of my sweatshirt, and gather the glass. I pick up at least a dozen pieces before I cut my finger. I stare at the blood a minute, until the tears start to form. I rush to the bathroom, turn the knob and place my finger under the warm water as it flows from the faucet, hoping the sounds of my sobs will get lost in the rush of water. Maybe if I can't hear them, it will be easier to stop.

The blood and water find their way to the sink separately, but liquid the color of watered down pink lemonade is speckled across the white marble basin. My chest heaves and I gasp, suffocating under the weight of my sobs.

I hear the front door close, and my tears stop abruptly. He's home early. I bring my hands halfway to my face in order to wipe my tears, then decide to leave them there. I am in this suspended animation when his face appears in the mirror behind me.

"Babe, what happened to your finger. Are you ok?"

Am I ok? Such a simple question. Such a logical question. I play out the conversation in my head. *"I cut my finger when I was cleaning up the glass." "Aw babe, you have to be more careful." He takes my hand in his... kisses my injured finger, and the day goes on. Maybe we order some food. We haven't had Chinese in a while. It's been a really long day though, might be a pizza and beer kinda night. He'll wrap his arms around me and we'll watch a movie, maybe a comedy, and I will forget.*

But today is not a simple day, and there is no logic for what has become of my life. I look down at the offending finger. Blood pools out and gets lost in the creases of my palm. I meet his eyes in the mirror and walk out without saying a word. I make it to the kitchen before he grabs my arm. My back still facing him, he speaks to me.

"What's up with you?"

I look over at the counter, empty milk carton, open cereal box. They bear witness. I hear Kiera's words in my mind, "This happened," and I turn on my heel. I square off my shoulders and set my jaw to mask my fear. I meet Aidan face to face and fix my mouth and my spirit to say the words.

With a quick jerk, I shrug his hand from my arm. I think it's his own genuine surprise at the motion, rather than the force I have exerted that causes him to release me.

"Do. Not. Touch. Me." I hear the sound of my words echo inside my head. They are quiet words, but strong words that don't betray my ever-escalating heart rate.

His eyes widen, and he takes a step back. His retreat makes me bold.

"Don't you *ever* touch me again," I walk past him, and we barely brush shoulders. I must go now before I lose my resolve. I stalk into my room, fling open the closet doors, yank my rolling suitcase down from the shelf, and throw it onto the floor. I make as much noise as I can, trying to project my emotions through the shift of every muscle, now that words have abandoned me.

I start throwing everything I own into the bag with little regard for how it's all going to fit, or where I will go once it's full. My vision is blasted with blouses in every color of the rainbow, sweatpants, jeans, winter coats and summer sarongs, business suits and cocktail dresses. When I shift to start on the shoes, I see him out of the corner of my eye. Just sitting there. On the end of the bed. Watching me. He looks sad. Why does he look like that? Why do I care that he looks like that? Don't you ask him Shae, don't you dare ask him. I bite down on my lip so hard I'm sure I draw blood. My mouth is full of questions. Just moments ago, it took everything I had to utter two sentences, and now here I am practically chewing my tongue to bits to keep from talking. The irony is not lost on me, and I chuckle to myself. He breaks the silence.

"Why are you laughing?"

I freeze. Should I answer his question? If I answer his question, those other words will fall out, and those are dangerous words that hedge on forgiveness and seep into forgetfulness, and I cannot afford either of those right now.

He stares at me, waiting for an answer. I remind myself I don't owe him an explanation. I don't owe him anything, but the sadness in his eyes goads me to answer him. If he had greeted me with arrogance or anger or sarcasm I would be able to ignore him, but his sadness softens me. I wonder if he knows this.

I give in.

"I'm laughing to keep from screaming. I'm laughing to remind myself what a ridiculous situation I find myself in. "

I meet his eyes. That is a mistake. "I am laughing because I am tired of crying." My voice breaks on the last word and makes me a liar.

He sees his opening and rises from the bed. He slowly drops to the floor, and inches toward me on all fours. In another situation the sight might have been comical.

I will not let him touch me. I will not let him touch me. I will not let him touch me. The mantra runs again and again in my head, picking up fervor the closer he gets. He is so close to me now, I can feel the warmth radiating off of his body, I must stop him before I can feel his breath on my skin. He reaches out a hand.

"No." I say.

He stops. I am surprised. He leans back, sits on his legs and places his hands in his lap.

"Can I just sit here next to you?"

"Ok." He moves a pair of pajamas and a red wool scarf that just missed the bag out of the way and scoots beside me. His proximity unnerves me. I shake under the pressure of unshed tears, unnamed emotions, and promises I have broken and will break to myself.

He reaches his arm out again, and this time I don't stop him. He drapes himself around me. He pulls me in close and I scream even though I am already crying. I beat my hands against his chest. He doesn't resist me. I am frustrated by how ineffectual my fists are and put more force behind my blows. I want him to hurt.

I pound on him until I am sweaty and sobbing. I collapse into his arms, defeated by the daunting prospect of changing my pattern.

The passing cars throw spears of light across the bedroom walls, breaking up the darkness, and leaving shadows in their wake. When the next car passes, I look down at Aidan's face, lying in the bed beside me. His features are completely relaxed. No tension hidden in the furrow of his brow, or the taut clench of his jaw. He never looks as soft as he does right now. Looking at him like this, I could almost believe that there is hope for us.

I slide to the edge of the bed using my hands to shift my weight while keeping the bed level. I place all of my weight in my toes, ease into the balls of my feet and then my heels creating a silent encounter with the hardwood beneath them. I look over my shoulder. Still sleeping. I tiptoe over to the sea of clothes still strewn all over the floor. I bend down and start picking them up, but I can't bring myself to put them back in the closet. I sink into sitting and settle for making neat piles of my folded wardrobe arranged by season.

I smooth my pants over my pants and hear a crinkle. I dig into my pocket, only to retrieve a piece of paper with a number scrawled across it. Kiera's number. These are my pants from another time, another life, and somehow only earlier today. I crane my neck and look at the glowing digits on the nightstand. 10:42. Late for a workday, but not super late. Too late to call? I chew on the cuticles of my thumb and index finger and mull it over. I strain to see the time again. 10:44. I'm on my feet.

I sit on the toilet seat with my knees tucked under my chin. I hold my cell phone with its shattered screen in my hands and say a prayer. I hold down the power button and it lights up. *Thank god.* I cradle it between my ear and my shoulder, as my fingers occupy themselves with picking at the already chipping paint on my toes. One ring. Two rings. Three rings, and I think about hanging up. Four rings.

"Hello?" A surprisingly chipper Kiera picks up the phone.

"Hi," is all I can muster.

"Shae, is that you?"

"It's me."

"Are you alright?"

I chuckle. "What's your definition of alright?"

I can hear the smile of her words, "Touché. Well, let's start with something more basic. Where are you?"

I hesitate. "I'm still here." I hang on the last word and wait for the judgment I know will come. I am embarrassed to have called this woman I barely know. Embarrassed to have shared the things that I have shared with her.

But, most of all embarrassed by my own weakness. I wish I were calling her from somewhere on the street, rolling my life in a suitcase behind me, unsure of where I will rest my head, but sure of my decision.

The smile has left her voice, but where I expected disappointment, I hear the reflection of my own sadness and confusion, "What happened?" she asks me.

I begin to recount the evening's events, detached, like I am reporting on the wreckage of somebody else's life. Kiera urges me on when I falter.

"I started off so strong, but then I just fell apart. I can't believe I'm still here. I can't believe I actually laid down in bed beside him expecting to go to sleep. This wasn't just some lover's quarrel, or a fight about who left the milk out on the counter..." my voice trails off.

"We all have to start somewhere Shae."

"But I can't stay here."

"No, you can't."

She is only repeating the same words I spoke a moment before, but her affirmation of them proves more powerful than my original utterance. It is as if I was only testing the waters when I said them, offering her the chance to give me an out, half hoping she would tell me I could stay.

We sit in silence on the phone, but it is not the awkward kind. I use this pause to rattle off all the permutations of where I can go from here. *Do I leave now, like right now, sneak out of my own home like a thief in the night? Do I wait til tomorrow and pack up while he's at work? Maybe I should wait until he comes home. Have my things all packed up and ready to go, but wait until he's here. Tell him why I'm leaving. Do I tell him why I'm leaving? I don't owe him an explanation, but do I need to tell him for some kind of closure? What if he tries to stop me? What will I do then? And where am I going when I leave?*

"Shae?"

It is only when I hear my name that I realize I've stopped breathing. I put the tirade of questions on hold, press my forehead to my knees and take a solid breath in and out.

"I think I have to leave now."

"Now? Like, right now?"

"Yeah. Right now. I think if I wait too long, I'll lose my nerve, and the way I'm feeling right now, even morning seems decades away."

"Ok, what can I do?"

"Can you, I mean, would you, if you can't it's totally alright..."

"Shae, just ask."

"Could you come meet me here? I think if I know you're here waiting for me, I'll feel like I have to leave. I won't want to make you come all this way and then stay."

"Of course I can do that. Do you want me to come up?"

"No, no, you don't need to come up."

I tell her the best subway lines and taxi routes to take, nice and easy, as if we're planning a chat over coffee and breakfast pastries, instead of my complete departure from life as I know it.

"Ok, I'm on my way, hang in there, ok?"

"Ok," I tell her.

After we hang up, I let the phone linger by my ear. I map out my next steps, in case I get lost inside myself along the way. *Throw on clothes. Put all the folded piles into the bag. Grab my purse. Throw in my cell phone, charger, wallet and keys. Wait… do I need my keys? I'm not coming back here, maybe I should leave the keys… If I take them does that mean something?* I don't have the space in my mind to ponder complicated concepts. Simplify. *Clothes. Bag. Purse.* I'll go on instinct. If my keys end up in the bag, they end up in the bag. If they don't, they don't.

Before I leave the bathroom, I go into my reserve stash of clothing, hoping to myself that this will be the last time I use them. I throw on yoga pants, sports bra, fitted t-shirt and some socks. As I pass through the hallway I snatch my hooded sweatshirt, pull it over my head, and lace up my running shoes.

In my room I transfer the piles of clothing into the bag, still wide open lying on the floor. Once they're in, I move on to all of the items still dangling from their hangers... too much to pack. I make snap judgments about what I will bring with me, and what gets left behind. It's amazing how easy it is to downsize when you haven't got a choice. I leave a few inches of space at the top, and fill up what remains with shoes. I zip up the main compartment and head to the small chest of drawers in the corner of the room. I drape a few pairs of tights around my neck, gather up half a dozen bras, two weeks worth of panties and a couple pairs of socks. I hear his voice behind me, before I turn and see him sitting up in the bed.

"What are you doing?"

I am only frozen for a breath, before I unhinge my feet from the floor and continue on my mission. I unzip the top flap of my bag, and start unloading my intimate apparel. I punctuate my words with my movements.

"I can't stay here."

He groans, "I thought we were past this."

"I'm not past anything."

"What happened between the time we went to bed and now?"

"I came to my senses."

"Come on Shae!"

I ignore him. I run my mental checklist again. Clothes. Check. Bag. Ready to go. Purse. Where's my purse?

"Shae! I'm talking to you!"

I vaguely register him sitting on the edge of the bed, grabbing a pair of sweatpants from off the floor. I jerk my bag upright, as my eyes dart around the room looking for my purse. There! It dangles from the doorknob of our room. He is standing up.

"You just gonna act like you don't hear me talking to you?"

I roll my bag behind me and snatch my purse from the door as I'm walking out. I check inside my bag. Wallet, phone, keys (I guess I will take the keys), charger? Charger? Shit! I think I left it inside the room. I hear his footsteps on the floor. Forget it, I'll get a new one.

"Would you just stop for a second?"

I am halfway down the hallway. I jerk backward as he grabs the strap of my purse.

"Just put these down so we can talk about this!"

I turn on my heel and yank my purse from his grasp. I summon a voice I didn't know I had from the bottom of my feet.

"You and I have *nothing* left to talk about."

He smiles as though my acknowledgement is a victory he can claim. "Oh, so you're talking to me now?"

"Talking to you long enough to say goodbye."

"Come on baby, you're not really leaving. Where you gonna go?"

"That's none of your concern, anywhere is better than here."

"So, that's it then. You're just gonna walk away? After all the years we've been together. Just like that?"

I mull over the years that I have spent in this relationship, getting further and further away from myself.

"I'm not walking away from you, I'm walking toward me." I say this in a whisper, but not because he frightens me, but because these words are for me.

"What?"

I speak up this time. "My leaving is not about *you*. It's not about you putting me down. It's not about you constantly treating me like I'm not good enough. It's not even about you raping me." I leave those words in the air for a moment. His mouth snaps shut, and he is stunned into silence. "My leaving is about me setting limits for myself. It's about me wanting more for myself.

It's about me putting myself first for once in my life. I am leaving for me, not you."

I take the keys out of my purse, and drop them on the ground before slamming the door behind me.

CHAPTER IV

I walk to the elevator with purpose. I step in and stand tall. I watch the numbers go down. Six, Five, Four, Three, Two, One, Lobby. I step out with a straight back and sure steps. It is not until after I nod to the doorman, refusing to acknowledge his puzzled look for more than a second, and step through the revolving door out into the crisp night air, that I show the vaguest sign of uncertainty or weakness.

I stop in front of the building so abruptly that the door hits my bag, which in turn hits me and I stumble. Where do I go now? I propel myself forward and just start walking. I cannot even remember whether I have turned left or right, uptown or downtown, headed east or west? I long for midday crowds where I can lose myself in the throngs of people, and let the tide of their movement carry me. The streets are too empty and the bright city lights feel like spot lights, highlighting my solitude.

My straight back curls, and my head bows forward. I walk with my eyes half closed, not even willing to make eye contact with the shadows. When my foot dips down in front of me I realize I have come to a curb and I look up. The sign says don't walk but the lack of traffic sends a different message. I step down and a car appears out of nowhere and cuts in front of me. With a sharp intake of breath, I retreat and decide to wait for the illuminated stick figure to guarantee me safe passage.

I hear a voice at my back shouting, but I don't realize that the woman is shouting my name until she places a hand on my shoulder. I jump at her touch.

"Shae, didn't you hear me calling you?" she asks.

"Kiera." I turn to her and register the kind face I only just discovered this afternoon.

"Hey."

"Hey."

"So, where ya headed?"

I look back over my shoulder. The sign glows with white light. The little man says its safe now, but how long has he been there? Will I make it to the other side, or will he betray me at the halfway point. I decide I cannot trust him.

"I don't know."

"Where were you walking?"

"I don't know; I just started to walk. I needed to move."

"I feel that."

She gives me the once over when she thinks I'm not paying attention. "Can I help you with your bag?"

I look down. I am clutching the handle of my bag as though it is the only thing keeping me tethered to the ground, the only thing that is keeping me from drifting off into some no-man's land for people like me who are somewhere between one life and the next.

When I don't respond to her she slides her hand over mine, and wiggles her fingers between my own. We stand like this for a minute looking at each other, fingers entwined holding the handle, and then I let go.

Kiera turns the corner rather than crossing the street. I watch her walk away rolling my life's possessions behind her. She notices my absence, reaches her free hand out behind her, and waits for me. I step forward and take her waiting hand. She is my anchor now.

We move like a unit drifting from one street to the next. She does not bother me with questions for which I have not even begun to think of answers. Occasionally she will squeeze my hand to let me know I have stopped moving or have slowed to the point where my motion is barely noticeable. I let the sound of the bag's wheels beating against the uneven pavement echo between my ears. As we walk I think about nothing and everything in shifts. When my own line of questioning becomes too much I let my mind go blank and settle back into the sound of the wheels and the warmth of Kiera's hand.

I am the one to break the silence. "We can not drift from street corner to street corner all night."

She feigns shock and confusion. "We can't???"

The tenor of her voice is reminiscent of Scooby Doo and it makes me laugh. I laugh so hard I double over, pulling her with me. My laugh travels through my arm and invades her body until we are both leaning against each other and my bag, fighting to stay upright.

"Why are we laughing?" She asks me in between gasps for air.

I choke out "I don't know," and for some reason this only sends us into further fits of hysteria.

The occasional passerby throw us dirty looks, but we barely notice them through our squinted eyes filled to the brim with jubilant tears.

I notice an ache in my belly, and the pain brings me back to reality. Kiera's cackles die down as she notices I have left our moment. She wipes tears from the corners of her eyes, and takes a steadying breath. She squeezes my hand.

I wait for her to speak. I wait for her to prompt me to think about what comes next. She doesn't. She sits on this street corner with me, as though it is the most natural thing in the world to do, holding my hand, sharing in my silence. There will be time for words later.

I stare up above me until the stars and the night sky blur together, and I am no longer sure what I am really seeing. I blink, and the world comes back into focus. If only everything in life were so easily fixed.

I bring my eyes back down from the heavens, and flex my free hand against the pavement. I don't think I've ever sat on the ground in the city before. I look at Keira sitting next to me. We must be a sight.

Despite the late hour we are not alone on the street. People pass us and make snap judgments that flit across their faces. Their pity, disgust, confusion and irritation are plain in their expressions. I choose to hone in on what is going on in their minds as a distraction from what is going on in my own.

"They probably think we're drunk."

"Say what now?

I realize I am having one of those moments where I have been involved in a silent conversation with myself, and don't realize I haven't given the outward dialogue a chance to catch up. I offer Kiera the Cliff Notes.

"I was just thinking about how we must look to other people on the street. It must seem weird, the two of us camped out on the ground like this, never mind all that laughing we were doing before."

"Honestly, I hadn't noticed, and I mean this is New York."

"But still, didn't see all those people walking by, looking at us like we were crazy."

"No, I guess not."

"Is that just now, or can you do that all the time?"

"Can I do what all the time?"

"Block out people staring at you, making faces, whispering in a way that's not really whispering, almost like they really want you to hear?"

"There was a time I noticed all of that, but you know what they say?"

"What's that?"

"What other people think of me is none of my business."

"It has never felt that simple for me."

"Well, think about it. Do any of these people on the street know you?"

"No."

"So then, what does their thinking one way or another about you really mean? What does it change? Do you look at yourself differently because some stranger doesn't approve of you?"

"I know the answer I'm supposed to give you, but honestly, the answer is yes."

"Really? Why does it matter to you?"

I have had the same talk with myself that Kiera is having with me now. When I walk down the street and some stranger looks at me sideways, I tell myself not to take it to heart. I tell myself these are strangers on the street who I've never seen before, and will likely never see again. But all of that is just words. Just an obligatory pep talk.

"You know, no one's ever asked me that before..."

"Asked you why you care what other people think?"

"Yeah. Although to be fair, I don't think I've ever told anyone about it before. I think I just kinda pretended it was something everybody did, so I never really had to think about why I do it. It's just something I do."

"Ok, so think about it now."

Kiera's eyes probe the side of my face as she waits for an answer. I think back to those people walking past us a few seconds ago. I remember the discomfort that started as a slight tightening in my chest, followed by a rush of warmth in my cheeks that would spread out to the tips of my ears. I play back the stream of thoughts set off by those feelings. I let a whoosh of breath escape my lips, and take a stab at her question.

"I think I'm looking for approval."

Kiera looks confused. "Approval from who?"

"From everyone."

"But, why?"

I look back up into the night sky and assume that intense focus until everything becomes a blur again. When I open my mouth to speak, I am talking to the sky as much as I am talking to Kiera. Or maybe these words are for me.

"The first beating I really remember happened when I was in Kindergarten... When you think of Kindergarten teachers, you think of warm, bubbly people doling out rainbows and unicorns and sunshine with every word... greeting their students in the morning with lollipops and hugs, making them each feel unique and valued... My Kindergarten teacher was more what you would expect of a prison warden."

I chuckle but it is empty.

"If that lady cracked a smile, nothing nice was following it."

I bring my eyes down from the sky and rest them on Kiera's face.

"Why do you suppose people do that?"

Kiera is justifiably confused, "Why do people do what?"

"Why do people spend their lives doing things that make them miserable?"

Kiera slowly shakes her head, "I don't know."

I furrow my brow and return to my conversation with the sky.

"Well, Mrs. Adams was clearly not excited to be teaching Kindergarten. In any case, one day when we were all supposed to be playing quietly with puzzles, one of the boys in my class told Mrs. Adams that I had failed to put all the puzzle pieces back in the box for this one particular puzzle of a forest or a jungle or something. Mrs. Adams called me up to the front of the class to stand next to the boy. Just before she started to talk she smiled, that should have tipped me off.

"Shae," she said with a slight lilt toward the end of my name, "Were you playing with this puzzle?"

"Yes, Mrs. Adams," I said.

"Are you done playing with it?"

"Yes, Mrs. Adams," I said again.

The smile disappeared, "Well, if you were done playing with it, why didn't you put all of the pieces back in the box?" Her words seemed to all end in sharp points.

I don't know how I managed to keep my voice steady, but perhaps at five I was stronger than I am two decades later.

"I did put all the pieces back Mrs. Adams," I told her.

She turned to the boy and asked him if he was sure there was a missing piece. The boy confirmed.

"I am going to write a note home to your mother to let her know that not only have you been having trouble following directions in class, but you're also having trouble telling the truth."

Despite having never been beaten at this point, I was terrified. Even then I did not doubt my mother's willingness to punish me. I begged my teacher not to write my mother a note.

"Please, Mrs. Adams, please don't write my mommy a note. Please. I really thought I put all the pieces back," I told her. "Maybe I dropped one and I didn't see. I'll look for it. I'll look for it right now," I told her.

She looked at me, but didn't respond. She simply opened the middle drawer in her desk, removed some stationary and began scrawling a note to my mother. The little boy who doomed me took the puzzle with its missing piece back to his desk and began assembling it again anyway in spite of its flaw.

I looked back and forth between Mrs. Adams and the boy, tears streaming down my face, and then ran to the back of the classroom where the puzzles were kept, determined to find the elusive puzzle piece and make everything right. I lifted up every puzzle box to see if it had fallen out onto the shelf. I opened the boxes of other puzzles I'd been playing with to see if I'd mistakenly put it in the wrong box.

I was running my hand underneath the shelf, and turning up nothing but dust bunnies when I heard Mrs. Adams.

"Shae, return to your seat."

I felt like I was on the verge of hysteria, but while I couldn't keep my tears from falling and my nose from running, I knew that any outburst might make my situation worse, so I choked back any panting or labored breathing that might have accompanied my sobs and took my seat.

Mrs. Adams walked over to my backpack and placed the note for my mother inside. After that she asked everyone to put away whatever they were playing with, and return to their seats.

My classmates shuffled around, placing things on and in shelves and bins. I heard the scrape of black, metal-legged chairs on the linoleum floor and knew they were taking their seats, even if I couldn't see them through my tears. And then a pause.

Mrs. Adams spoke again, "Yes, Eva."

Eva spoke, "Mrs. Adams, I see the missing puzzle piece under his chair."

I blinked enough to see what was going on. Eva was pointing at the floor under the seat of the boy who'd accused me, and sure enough there was the puzzle piece.

Mrs. Adams walked over and picked it up. She said, "Would you look at that."

That's it. That's all she said. She didn't bring me back up to her desk to apologize. She didn't even offer me a tissue to wipe my face. And most tragically, she didn't take that note out of my backpack.

The whole walk home, I kept hoping that she'd slipped it out at some point when I wasn't paying attention. But when my mother called me out of my room in less time than it took me to take off my uniform and put on my play clothes, I was shaking. I knew that note was still in my backpack and she had seen it.

My mother stood in the kitchen with her back to me, drumming her fingers on the note lain out on the kitchen counter. Without turning around to face me she said, "Shae, is there something you would like to tell me?

I started picking at my cuticles and chewing on my bottom lip, nervous habits I've had for as long as I can remember. I looked down at my feet.

"Shae, do you hear me talking to you?" Her words were crisp but quiet.

"Yes, Mommy."

"Well then answer my question."

"The teacher, I mean Mrs. Adams, um."

"Don't say um."

"Mrs. Adams, uh, I mean, this boy in my class."

"Get to the point."

"It was a mistake. I put all the puzzle pieces in the box. Mrs. Adams was supposed to take the note out of my bag, but she must have --" before more words could tumble out, my mother spun around and cut me off.

"Don't you lie to me."

"I'm not lying, Mommy! That's what happened, Mommy. I promise." I begged her to believe me.

She spun back around and started rummaging through the cabinets close to the floor. She emerged with a small wooden cutting board that had a handle, turned around, grabbed my arm and marched me into my room. With her free hand she closed the windows and the blinds. She sat on my bed. I stood in the doorway, as far away from her as I could manage and still be respectful.

"What do I send you to school for?" she asked me.

"To learn."

"Do I send you there to embarrass me?"

"No, Mommy."

"Do I send you there to show your ass and act up?"

"No, Mommy." My body began to tremble and my hands began to sweat.

"I raised you better than to be a liar."

"I didn't lie, Mommy, I didn't--"

"Shut your mouth."

"You are too old to be acting like you don't know better. But if you want to be hard-headed, that's fine with me. We'll get that straightened out in no time. Come stand in front of me."

Terrified though I was, I quickly did as she asked lest I make things worse by dragging my feet.

"Turn around, and pull down your pants," she said."

A rogue tear rolls down my cheek as I remember what comes next. I chew on the inside of my cheek to stop the others that threaten to follow it and finish my story.

"I tried to bite on my tongue to keep myself from crying out because I was afraid if I made noise it would make her more mad. But after a little while, I couldn't help it. I screamed. I swore to her I wasn't a liar. When insisting on my innocence didn't work I tried a new tactic. I promised her I would be good from now on. I told her I would do better. I begged her to stop.

When hysteria finally took over, I began to cry out, "Mommy, please," like a mantra. When she stopped, I didn't even notice at first because the throbbing in my backside was so intense."

"Jesus, Shae, you were five when that happened? Five?"

I look over at Keira staring at me wide-eyed, "Yeah," I answer her.

She shakes her head. "I know when we're little our parents are all omniscient and can do no wrong in our eyes, but looking back on that, you have to see how fucked up that was."

"For the most part I do, but, it took me a long time to get there, and sometimes I feel like I can't take back the impression that growing up like that left on who I am. When you're a kid and you constantly hear how much of an embarrassment you are, and all the different ways you're just not good enough, it becomes you. When you know some random person's idle observation of you can get you beaten so badly..." My words trail off. "You become everything they say. I remember the first time one of my teachers told me I was gifted, smart. I hung on that compliment for hours. For a little while I got to live in that image of who my teacher thought I was instead of that other girl... the disappointment. At some point without even realizing I was doing it, I started to live for those moments, you know, live for those compliments, those random kindnesses doled out by strangers."

"So, when you see people on the street, and they look like they're..."

"Passing judgment? Disapproving of me in some way? It has the opposite effect of the compliments. When strangers look at me that way, it means people who don't even know me can see the things I've been told since I was a little girl. They can see my inadequacy, my weakness and they don't even know my name."

Kiera shakes her head.

I change the subject. "Did I tell you I went to Catholic school til I was in 3rd grade?" I tell her.

"Nope, you didn't mention that." Kiera doesn't miss a beat, no longer phased by my vacillating train of thought.

"Yup. St. Joseph's."

"I don't know much about the saints."

"Ya know, I don't either, and I probably should." I laugh. "The thing I remember most about being in Catholic school was learning how to pray." I look over at her. "I was a little... I believed in God the way kids believed in Santa Claus. I thought I could make a list and pray for it, and God would deliver, as long as I was a good girl."

"What did you pray for?"

"I prayed for him to make me a better person so I wouldn't make my mom mad all the time. I prayed that my father would come back so we could be a family, me, him and my mom. I thought that might make my mom happy too. I thought it would be nice to stop the endless stream of boyfriends and have someone who would stick around for a while. I prayed for money, so my mom wouldn't have to make so many sacrifices for me... I prayed and I prayed and I prayed. I would beg God to hear me, the way I would beg my mother not to beat me. But it seemed God wasn't listening any more than she was."

Kiera places her hand in the middle of my back and rubs in gentle clockwise circles that get wider and wider as I speak.

"I can't imagine growing up like that," she tells me.

"You know what, stuff like that wasn't even the hardest part of it all. It was that she wasn't like that all the time. One day I'd get home from school, she'd greet me with a smile, say "Hey baby girl," pull me into her lap, rake her fingers through my hair and kiss me gently on my forehead. I'd close my eyes and say another prayer that she could be like this always. But the very next day I'd come home and she wouldn't even make eye contact with me. I'd go to give her a hug and she'd shrug me away. Everything I did would come with a critique down to the way I chewed my food at dinner."

I rested my elbow against my knee and propped up my chin with my fist.

"There was no rhyme or reason to it either... Each day I would wake up and wonder what will she be like today, and just because she woke up one way wouldn't mean she'd stay that way, so I'd have to wonder the same thing on my way home from school. And it was like that the entire time I was growing up. I never knew if my mother loved me, but I spent every day trying to at least make her like me. I was always anxious, always second-guessing everything I did. I don't think I ever opened my mouth to speak without running the words over in my head two or three times before releasing them into the world. And it wasn't just at home. The way I was with her bled into the way I was everywhere, until that's just who I was... anxiety ridden and riddled with self-doubt."

Kiera scoots closer to me and places an arm around my shoulders.

"Sometimes I just feel so broken. Like there's no fixing the damage I've got. Like I have zero shot at being normal."

"But what is normal?" Keira stops rubbing my back a moment as she asks this question.

"What?" I ask her. Now I am the one who is thrown off.

"What is normal? When you say you have zero shot at being normal, what does that mean? What does normal look like?"

I tilt my head back and furrow my brow. "I don't know that I've ever stopped to think about what normal *looks* like. I associate it with a feeling..."

"Ok, so what does normal *feel* like?"

"Normal feels like, like being comfortable in your own skin. Like knowing that you're going to make some mistakes, and get some things wrong, but being ok with that. Normal feels like not constantly worrying that the people in your life are upset with you, or that they're going to abandon you. Normal feels like being able to tell people how you're really feeling and what you're thinking, instead of always just saying what you think you're supposed to say. Normal feels whole, like being a whole person, and not just pieces of a person all the time."

Kiera doesn't say anything. I look at her face out of the corner of my eye and it is thoughtful. I turn to face the street, and we fall back into a comfortable quiet. I think people are mistaken when they place quiet at odds with the existence of sound. It may not be as abrasive as noise or as commanding as loud, but quiet has a sound. It is a low hum. It is the sound when no other sound exists that lets you know you're alive. The absence of sound is nothing and quiet is not nothing.

Kiera takes her arm from around my shoulders and grabs my free hand.

"Well honey, you're never gonna be normal if we don't get off the street." She smiles and the warmth of that smile spreads to my face and I am grinning in spite of myself.

"You're forgetting one thing," I tell her.

"What's that?"

"I don't know where I'm going."

She rolls her eyes and squeezes my hand.

"You're coming home with me, duh."

I think about arguing with her. I think about telling her she doesn't know me from a hole in the wall. I think about insisting that it's too much of an imposition. But all I say is, "Ok."

CHAPTER V

I am breathless when we arrive at the top of Kiera's fifth floor walkup. "Welcome to my penthouse suite," she winks at me and pushes the door open.

The walls alternate between molten yellow marigold, and the bright cheery red of freshly bloomed poppy flowers. Her furniture is a hodge podge of woods in different stains, modern, vintage, simple and ornate. Tie-dyed fabrics and cloths printed with West African Adinkra symbols adorn the frames of her floor length windows in lieu of curtains, drawing attention away from the bars separating the open air and her apartment. The air is thick with the smell of sandalwood and jasmine, as I quickly locate the empty incense holder in the middle of her coffee table covered in ash that spills out over covers of half read magazines and open notebooks full of sketches and thoughts saved for later. Kiera's apartment is an extension of herself, and it hums with her energy and warmth.

I realize I have been standing there, staring, and I blurt out the first thing that comes to mind, "I love your apartment."

She slides my suitcase up against the couch and smiles. "Let me give you the grand tour."

She fans her arms out on either side of her. "This as you can see is my living room, and for the time being, your room."

She walks about five paces and sits on an oak stool at the bar overlooking her kitchen. "This is where I eat my meals, and that is where I occasionally cook them," she said pointing across the counter.

Seconds later we turn down a short hallway. At the first door on the left she pushes in a door to reveal the bathroom, the second door holds a linen closet, from which she retrieves some supplies for my stay, and the last door holds her room.

She flips a switch and once again, I am lost in the intricacies of how a person becomes their space. A purple cloth draped over a lamp bathes the room in a permanent sunset. Pictures and postcards and magazine clippings and drawings cover every inch of the wall opposite her bed. The ceiling is a tapestry of glow in the dark stars arranged to reflect actual constellations. Her wardrobe from the past week is strewn on top of the trunk at the foot of her bed, and in pockets here and there on the floor.

No words come to mind so I just smile.

"Come," she tells me, "You must be exhausted."

I sit in a rocking chair opposite her, and watch as she places a fluffy turquoise towel and hot pink washcloth on the end table nearest the couch. I feel my head begin to nod in time with the chair as she tucks a sheet up under the couch cushions, and fluffs a pillow for me to rest my head. When I jerk myself awake, I pause, disoriented by the time I must have lost. The room is dark now, the couch is now also outfitted with a sheet and there are pajama shorts and an old t shirt laid out over the pillow. I am covered in a light cotton blanket, and my shoes are no longer on my feet.

I look at my suitcase and think about digging out something of my own to sleep in, but I don't want to cause a ruckus and wake Kiera, so I shimmy out of the rest of my attire and put on what she has offered me. I look around for a clock or a microwave or anything that will tell me what time it is. I think about searching for my purse in the dark, so I can check my cell phone, and then decide it doesn't matter. Time will still be here in the morning. So, I pull back the sheets and slip into my makeshift bed.

I am surprised how easily sleeps comes again, in the home of this woman I didn't know 24 hours ago. I listen to my breath even out, listen to it lengthen and deepen. I am too tired for worry, too tired even for my subconscious to drum up images from today and transform them into nightmares, and so I sleep soundly in a place where my memories can't find me, and the pain that comes along with them can't hurt me.

I open my eyes and am struck with early morning amnesia. As I hang in the space between sleeping and waking I am embraced by a fleeting peace fueled by my temporary ignorance. I am in neither today nor tomorrow. I am barely aware that I have a body and my name is nothing more than a vague notion. In this space dreams are more vivid than reality and I toy with the idea that perhaps yesterday was nothing more than a nightmare. But all of that happens in a second, and as my surroundings become solid, anxiety settles in where peace once lived.

Kiera is already awake. She runs down her schedule briefly before leaving a spare key on the kitchen counter and running out the door with an English muffin hanging out of her mouth clenched between her teeth. I hear her through a fog, only picking up on the important parts. Gone til 4. Keys on the counter. Call if you need anything.

I latch on to that last bit. *Call if you need anything.* If I *need* anything. What do I need right now? I am sporting bed head and crusty eyes in the home of a woman I met just yesterday, and all of my belongings, or at least all of what I've decided to hold on to, is in a suitcase next to the coffee table. Surely I must need something.

I wrinkle my nose at the smell of fresh brewed coffee and search Kiera's cabinets for tea. It comes down to Chai or English Breakfast. Chai wins. I drift through Kiera's house like a ghost, mug in one hand, empty fingers trailing over countertops and across walls. I open the window and sit, looking down below. I watch people. I watch traffic. I watch life and try to breath it in. I watch everything continue and wonder if they can feel the shudder of this butterfly's wing that has felt so monumental to me. Does the light look different to any of them today? Does the ground feel different underneath their feet?

I turn away from the window and look at Kiera's apartment without really seeing it. I walk over to the countertop, put down the mug, and palm the spare key. I find my purse, dig inside and retrieve my phone. 8:30am. I run my thumb over the key in my hand. If I hurry I can still make it on time ... Couldn't hurt to try.

It is surprisingly easy to return to work. No one looks at me any differently. They have no reason to suspect anything other than either I was sick or playing hooky, or had some other benign reason for being absent yesterday. The clock in the center of my desk reads 9:12am, when I plop down into my chair... hardly late enough to raise any eyebrows. I'm barely halfway through my new emails when it's time for lunch. I walk to the corner coffee shop with Lily. She brings me up to speed on the latest gossip. I laugh and gasp in all the right places while tearing off little bite sized pieces of my fancy $9 sandwich that occasionally make it to my mouth. I sip my fresh squeezed lemonade and nod thoughtfully as Lily hops from office gossip, to personal gossip, to *The Real Housewives of...* somewhere. Her expression gives me no indication that I have missed a single beat.

Thankfully I have no crucial appointments today, just a staff meeting populated by enough people that I am able to fade into the background with little to no effort. Outside of that I fall back into the cadence of checking email and sending responses. It is as though I have flipped a switch and am running an auto pilot program in my mind. This may be a horrible coping mechanism, but my mind is busy and I am grateful for that. I am grateful for the legitimate excuse not to have to think. I hone in on my computer until the rest of my office fades away, and there is only it and me.

I people watch on the subway ride back to Kiera's. I make up their destinations and origins and even choose their favorite colors. By the time I reach Kiera's stop I know these strangers so well I am tempted to introduce myself, and compare my fictional notes with reality.

Kiera's face brightens when I walk in the door as if she is surprised to see me there. Funny, it never occurred to me to come anywhere but here. She fans out take-out menus on the countertop and tells me her kitchen is mostly for show. We waffle between Japanese and Chinese a while, and finally decide on sushi and seaweed salad.

"So..." Kiera leads the conversation

"So?"

"So... how about those Yankees?"

"Seriously?"

We laugh.

Kiera starts back in, "But for real, how was your day?"

"Eh, you know, it was a day, how was yours?"

"It was pretty good. I met with a few potential clients, booked a couple speaking engagements, waded through some emails...productive day."

I start to open my mouth to speak a few times but close it when I can't figure out how to phrase what I want to ask.

Kiera squints at me, "So, you actually gonna speak at some point or what?"

I let out a trill of nervous laughter.

"Ok, so you said you're your own boss, and you just said something about clients, but, what is it that you do exactly"

Kiera laughs, "I guess that never really came up, huh?'

"Nope, not so much."

"Well, it always seems kinda cheesy to say it this way, but I guess the easiest way to explain what I do is to say I'm a life coach. Really, I just help people get out of their own way."

"Cool, so am I like a pro-bono case or something?"

Kiera gives me half of a smile, "Yeah, something like that."

We sit in silence moving food around our plates, each lost in our own thoughts. Kiera breaks the silence with a question.

"Can I ask you a question."

"I think you already are."

She shoves my shoulder, "You know what I mean."

I smile, "Go ahead."

"You talk a lot about your mom."

"Yeah."

"So, where is she now?"

"I don't know."

"You don't know? I mean I figured things were rocky. You're here after all, and not with her, but you don't even know where she is?"

I let out a long sigh.

"She called me this one time, telling me about her latest boyfriend. Telling me how awful he was. Telling me how he would beat her... I'd never really said anything when she told me about her boyfriends before. I usually just listened, and said what I knew she wanted to hear, and, I don't know what made me say it, but, I told her to leave. I told her to leave him"

I laugh, at the irony, "Funny right... here I am tellin' her to leave somebody... in any case, I told her to leave. Told her to come stay with me and Aidan. This was right after we'd first moved in together. That was before, well, just before..."

"So, what happened?"

"She got it into her head that I was looking down on her. That I was asking her to come stay with me because I pitied her or something. She said "What, you think you're some kinda relationship expert now? You think this won't happen to you and Aidan one day? They all turn on you at some point, ain't you learned that by now. You can't trust anybody. Least of all a man."

I tried to tell her it didn't have to be like that. I tried to tell her she didn't have to resign herself to that, that she deserved better, but it was like she couldn't hear me. and before I knew it, she was shouting at me. Telling me to lose her number. Telling me to never call her again."

"Did you? Call her I mean."

"I tried. It always went straight to voicemail. I kept trying, but then one day the number had changed... For a little while I tried to bump into her in the neighborhood where her boyfriend lived. One day I even mustered up the courage to ring her bell, but strangers answered."

"So you have no idea where she is?"

"I assume she's still somewhere in New York, but who knows."

"You think maybe you'll try to find her again one day?"

"Maybe...you know I never imagined she would do this to me. I'd seen her do it countless people growing up. Friends, boyfriends, the family members I never got to meet. She didn't even keep a job for very long, so even her co-workers were always changing... but I never imagined she'd do this to me. I thought I was different."

I pick at my cuticles and avoid Kiera's eyes.

She places her hand over mine. "I think that's enough heavy conversation for the evening, don't you."

I bring my eyes up to meet hers and offer a weak smile. "I'd say so."

"Let's see what's on TV."

We watch syndicated episodes of childhood favorites, *The Fresh Prince* and *Family Matters* on my makeshift bed. The opening credits for *A Different World* come on, Kiera glances at the time, and we both realize it is past our bedtime. She says goodnight, and I stay behind to stare at the ceiling until my eyes feel like closing.

I make it a week like this. Wake up. Go to work. Come back. Have dinner with Kiera. Watch TV or a movie. Go to bed. Rinse and Repeat. On the weekend I am glued to Kiera's couch. She says things to me about sunshine, fresh air and Vitamin D, but I poo poo all of that. I lose hours between cartoons and old sitcoms and made for TV movies. I am sure this is some stage of grieving but I don't care. The only world that exists outside of Kiera's house is in my office, and if I don't have to go there, I won't go anywhere.

Monday comes and I begin my cycle again. Ready to continue on like this indefinitely, but then, the flowers show up. I wake up. I go to work, and there in the middle of my desk, like they've always been there, in a simple glass vase, are peonies in every shade of pink imaginable.

I close the door to my office behind me, and lean up against it, as far from the peonies as I can manage. At first I worry that he dropped them off himself, but quickly tell myself that's silly. Surely he had the florist drop them off. All the same, I open back up the door to my office and peek down the hall. The coast is clear.

What does he expect me to do with these? I sit at my desk, eyeing up my favorite flowers for the traitors that they are. I notice a small white envelope tucked in amongst the blooms, and against my better judgment, decide to read the note:

"Miss you. Love you. Come home."

Miss you, love you, come home? Is that really the best he could do? I scold myself for thinking, however briefly, that he might actually put an admission of wrong-doing in writing. Silly me. Not like he has anything to apologize for! Not that I want his apology. We are beyond I'm sorry. I fight the urge to sweep my arm across the desk, knocking the vase to the floor where it would surely shatter.

I drum my fingers on my desktop. I pick up my phone. No, I will not call him. There is no coming back from that, and that's exactly what he wants me to do. I stare at the flowers another minute, then pick them up, walk out of my office and hand them to Lily.

"Can you put these in the Mosley Memorial Conference Room for me, please?"

She looks confused, but she doesn't pry. "Sure," she says.

I walk back into my office, proud at how well I handled flowergate. I spend the rest of the day only mildly obsessing over Aidan's attempt to reconcile.

As I stand on the platform waiting for the train, my phone chimes in one low note, letting me know I have an incoming text message. I wonder what Kiera has in mind for dinner tonight, but instead:

Did you get the flowers?

Did I get the flowers? Did I get, the flowers? Did I, get the flowers. Did I get. The flowers. Did. I. Get. The. Flowers. I go over the line over and over in my head until it starts to sound like gibberish.

When I walk into Kiera's apartment, she is standing in the hallway and I thrust my phone at her in lieu of a greeting. She gives it a glance, looks up, raises an eyebrow and says, "He sent flowers?" She walks over and sits on the couch.

I plop down next to her, "Yeah. Would it be rude for me not to let him know I got them?"

"Rude? Seriously Shae, rude?"

"I'm just asking! It wouldn't mean anything if I typed back "yes," just one word. Three little letters. Nothing deep, just "yes.""

"And then what?"

"And then what, what?"

"And then when he texts you back and asks you if you like them, is it gonna be rude for you to not answer that too? And what about all the questions that come after that? Where are you? When are you coming back? What about those questions, Shae?"

I stare at her blankly. She sits waiting. When I still don't respond, she places her hand on my cheek, and then moves it to my knee.

She says, "He's looking for an opening. Any opening. Don't give him one." She looks at me one more moment then heads back to her room.

I sit on the couch, shoes still on, bag still slung over my shoulder, key ring still wrapped around my finger, and the phone still clutched in my grasp.

I unlock the screen and open my text messages. I close them and open them again. I lock the screen, unlock it. Place the phone on the couch next to me. My knee is jumping. I tap my foot on the floor. I hear the door to Kiera's room open. Hear the water turn on. I pick up the phone, walk into the kitchen. Grab a mug. Fill it with water, and drop the phone inside. What a shame. Cracked screen. Water damage. Looks like I'll have to get a new phone, and while I'm at it, I might as well get a new number. I smile at the drowning device, proud of myself. I leave it on the counter, and try not to give it a second thought.

When I walk into the office the next morning, I peek around the door slowly, unsure of what I may find on the desk today, but it is empty. I sit down at my desk relieved and open up my email. There in the 20th line from the top, though it may as well have popped up first waving a red flag, is an email from Aidan. The subject line reads: *Did you get the flowers?* I click on it, and there is no content. Just that one line again. I block his email address before I have time to think about it.

All day my nerves are on edge. I don't know what I am waiting for, and that just makes it worse. When I make it to 5:00pm without incident, I start to relax, and by Friday, I have settled back into my routine. Wake up. Go to work. Come back. Have dinner with Kiera. Watch TV or a movie. Go to bed. Rinse and Repeat.

When I get to work Lily greets me with a smile and a chai tea latte. I return her smile, and thank her for the pleasant surprise, but am not prepared for the surprise sitting behind my desk.

I would have preferred an office full of peonies over what waits for me there.

Aidan sits with his hands clasped in his lap. He wears a gray suit, deep purple tie, and a stern expression. The smile falls from my face and it is a wonder I don't drop the chai too. I hear Lily say something to me, but she sounds like she is talking through a tunnel. I look back over my shoulder at her.

"What?" I ask her, voice strained.

"I said, sorry. He said he wanted to surprise you."

I want to scream. I want to tell her bringing me a chai is a nice surprise. Realizing we have Monday off, and it's a long weekend is a nice surprise. Finding Aidan in my office is not a nice surprise. Then I realize I've been so caught up in going through the motions, and keeping up with my routine that I've neglected some details. I didn't tell Lily that Aidan and I were over. She didn't know. So I choke on my screams, thank her, and close the door behind me.

"What are you doing here?" I ask him.

"Where are they?"

"Where are what?"

"Don't get cute Shae. The flowers. Where are they?"

I shrug.

"Lily told me you got them."

"Well obviously they're not here."

"You know, it's common courtesy, when someone gives you something, to say thank you. But at the very least, you let them know you got it."

"And what makes you think I owe you common courtesy?"

Aidan closes his eyes and his nostrils flare. He touches his forehead to his clasped hands.

"I have work to do, so if you could see yourself out..." I am matter-of –fact and to the point.

His head snaps up, "Really?" He chuckles. "I should see myself out, huh?" He gets up out of the chair and walks around to the front of my desk. I put one hand on the doorknob.

"I would hate to have you escorted from the building."

He licks his lips and smiles. He buttons his suit jacket, and tosses his shoulders back.

"You don't have to have me escorted from anywhere. Are you gonna come by to get the rest of your shit, or should I just leave it out on the curb?"

I stand tall and meet his eyes. "I have everything I need."

I release the doorknob and slide to the side so he can leave. Just before he leaves he turns to me. "You think you can do better than me?"

Words fail me.

"You're doing me a favor. It's about time I cut you loose anyway." He flips a switch, turns on a smile, and waves to Lily as he makes his way to the elevator.

I slide down the wall and sit on the floor, up against the wall, near the door. *Is he right? Can I do better than him? What am I doing? Am I making a mistake. Maybe I should –*

"No." I don't realize I've spoken aloud, and apparently quite forcefully, until Lily knocks lightly on the door.

"Are you alright?"

"No," I say quietly to myself, "but I will be."

Lily knocks again and I say more audibly, "I'm ok."

I get up on my feet, and put my hand on the door. I think about waiting thirty minutes, waiting until I'm sure he's gone and I won't run into him, and then I realize I don't care.

CHAPTER VI

I cross my legs on the park bench and breathe in the fresh air. My hands have almost stopped shaking. I shrug off my blazer and take long, slow, deep breaths. I think about calling Kiera, but decide against it.

I pull my legs out from underneath me, slip out of my shoes and walk through the grass. The ground is warm underneath my feet. Tears fall down my face and I make no effort to wipe them away. These are the tears of a new beginning.

I walk until the sun has dried my face, take out the compact from my bag to study my features in the mirror, and sit under the shade of a tree. My eyes are puffy, but not red. There is a little moisture underneath my nose, but nothing you would notice unless you were looking. And then there are things I don't know that anyone but me would see. There is a twinkle in my eye that I didn't see there before, and a glow in my skin despite the hint of tear stains here and there.

I let out a whoosh of air and note that my shoulders don't feel so heavy and my chin sits a little higher than it did this morning.

I close the compact, slip on my shoes and stand up. I look to the sky. The sun has risen higher from when I first left the office. It's no longer morning. I lower my eyes, step onto the path and set out into the afternoon.

ABOUT THE AUTHOR

When Satya was a little girl, she wanted to be everything under the sun: a teacher, a pilot, a firefighter, a lawyer, the President, a detective in the Special Victims Unit (thank you Law and Order), and a writer. Always a writer. No matter how everything else on that list might have changed, writer always stuck.

Writing helped her find her voice, and sharing that voice with others is both the most terrifying and most exciting thing she has ever done.

15635930R00076

Made in the USA
Middletown, DE
14 November 2014